This book

belongs to:

....

....

Published by Honey Bunny Books, an imprint of Brisance Books Group LLC
Honey Bunny Books is a trademark owned by Diane Kwon.

The publisher is not responsible for websites or their content that are not owned by the publisher.
Honey Bunny Books may be purchased in bulk at special discounts for sales promotion, corporate gifts, fundraising, or educational purposes.

Brisance Books Group for Honey Bunny Books
21001 N. Tatum Blvd.
Phoenix, AZ 85050

Visit HoneyBunnyBooks.com

Printed in the United States of America
First Edition: March 2021
Hardcover ISBN: 978-1-944194-76-5
Illustrations by Marina Martin
Diane Kwon portrait credit: Gareth Conway and Marina Martin
Cover design and interior production by PCI Publishing Group LLC

Oinkree and the Dancing Ant

DIANE KWON
ILLUSTRATED BY MARINA MARTIN

For the little girl
dreaming under the baby grand piano
&
For every child who wants to find a friend
and needs a little courage
Kent & Kaia, I Love You Infinity
– D.K.

To Noa, I hope you face the world with courage, enjoy a thousand adventures, and then
come home loaded with stories.
&
To Javi, who will listen to them by my side.
– M.M.

Oinkree was a nervous chap who rarely went outside.
He spent his days in his warm, cozy home
eating jars of Snuffle Jam.

1

Oinkree wished he could go on adventures,
but he was afraid of almost everything!

Ride a scooter?
What if I fall into a pothole?

Go to the beach?
What if a crab pinches my toes?

Go skiing?
What if I tumble down a hill?

Oinkree's life was lonely, but as Grandmama always used to say,
"Oinkree! Better afraid and safe than brave and sorry!"

Then one day, Oinkree had a great shock!
He opened the kitchen cabinet and found
that all the shelves were empty!

"Oh no!" Oinkree cried as he fell to the floor.

He knew what he had to do.

He had to go outside to collect Snuffle berries or else he would have no food.

Oinkree stood in front of the door and thought,
"I *really* don't want to do this!"

His hands were sweaty, and he felt like fainting,
but he picked up his basket and counted,

"One,

two,

three!"

With that, he took a deep breath,
pulled the door open, and ran toward the woods.

The day was sunny but eerily quiet.
Oinkree looked from left to right.

Surely something was hiding in the bushes!
Certainly, something was watching him!

Could it
be a tiger?

Could it
be a bear?

Maybe a
feisty squirrel?

Oinkree walked
faster and faster!
He was very scared.

Finally, he saw a field of bushes filled with many Snuffle berries.

"Whew! There it is! Snuffle Berry Place Clearing!" Oinkree said.

His little heart started cheering.

Oinkree placed his basket down
and reached for a ripe berry.

Just then he heard a tiny voice.

"Hello! What are you doing?" it asked.

Oinkree spun around,
but there was no one there!
"Wh-who made that sound?" he said.

Then...

*crunch, crunch
crunch!*

He heard
munching
close
to his ear.

Oinkree looked at his shoulder and saw a little creature
sitting there. It was eating a Snuffle berry
and looking very jolly.

"Ahhhh! A stranger! Please don't hurt me!" cried Oinkree.
"I am hungry and just wanted some berries.
Please let me go!"

"Hungry, you say? I could help you if you come on out!" said the tiny creature. "Let me introduce myself. Then I won't be a stranger anymore!"

Oinkree stood as still as a statue.

"You are a million times my size. There's no need to scream and hide. You don't have to be afraid!"

"Help me?"

Oinkree thought for a
minute and looked over
at the little creature.

"He seems friendly,
and he *is* tiny.
What have I got to lose?"

Oinkree got up and took a step forward.

"Nice to meet you!" said the small creature, bowing. "I am a Dancing Ant, and I have a special power. I can help you with the Snuffle berries if you promise not to run away."

Oinkree nodded.

The Dancing Ant said, "Okay!
Then hold up your basket
and stand by!"

All of a sudden, the ant started dancing,
hopping up and down, and spinning.
He chanted,
"Kazoo Kazoo Alamazoo. Kazoo Kazoo CHA-HA!
 Kazoo Kazoo Alamazoo. Kazoo Kazoo CHA-HA!"

The ground started moving, and the leaves started shaking. Oinkree looked up and was surprised!

One by one, the Snuffle berries fell straight into his basket!

The Dancing Ant yelled, "Let's collect more berries.
I have a few friends who can help!"

Thump, thump, thump!

He tapped his foot on the ground and shouted, "CHA-HA!"

Then suddenly,
from underground,
a group of ants came
out in a conga line.

They all chanted,
"Kazoo Kazoo Alamazoo. Kazoo Kazoo CHA-HA!
  Kazoo Kazoo Alamazoo. Kazoo Kazoo CHA-HA!"

Berries started falling all around.

"This is so amazing!"
Oinkree said aloud.
"It's not scary…it's great!"

Oinkree felt someone tap his foot.
It was the Dancing Ant.

The ant twirled around quickly and said, "Join us!
Let's all dance together!"

Then the strangest thing happened.

Oinkree wiggled his body!
He put his hands in the air
and started dancing too!

As he was laughing and spinning,
Oinkree felt the corners of his mouth move.

He shouted,

"KAZOO KAZOO
ALAMAZOO.

KAZOO KAZOO
CHA-HA!"

Then, with a thunderous crash, all the Snuffle berries fell at once in a gigantic pile. Oinkree was covered.

He popped his head up and looked for the Dancing Ants.

"Hello?! Are you there? Dancing Ants, can you hear me?"
He wanted to find his friends fast!

Immediately, to his right, he heard a little giggle.
He looked down and saw the Dancing Ant.

Oinkree's heart warmed, and his eyes twinkled.
He picked up the ant and placed him on his shoulder.

Then Oinkree saw the other ants climbing
out of the pile of berries one by one.

Oinkree smiled and said,
"Thank you for your kindness. Will you join
me for lunch? I would love the company
if you don't mind walking a while."

The Dancing Ant hugged Oinkree, and the
other ants shouted, "Lead the way!"

As they walked, they pointed at butterflies, told funny stories, and tried to catch flying dragonflies.

When they arrived at Oinkree's warm, cozy home, the new friends made jars of Snuffle Jam together. With so many helping hands, it took no time at all to fill the kitchen shelves.

Then everyone sat around the table and feasted
on jam and toast until their bellies were full.

Oinkree looked around his home.
"What a wonderful day!" he said to himself.
"New things are not as scary as I thought.
The path seems friendlier and the world seems kindlier
when you have a few good friends to share adventures with."

With that, Oinkree picked up the Dancing Ant
and placed him on his shoulder.

Then, they both snuggled into Oinkree's favorite armchair
and enjoyed a delicious afternoon nap.